P9-BIQ-766

SUDDEN SECRETS

MEG CARAHER

Illustrated by Tony Pyrzakowski

DISCARD

Rigby

For my dear brother and sisters—
Michael, Claire, and Ruth,
with love.

Thank you to Eddie Rua,
whose courage and humor
inspired this story.

CONTENTS

CHAPTER 1

A Great Swim   1

CHAPTER 2

Will's Story   6

CHAPTER 3

A Surprising Turn   10

CHAPTER 4

A Secret Revealed   14

CHAPTER 5

The Secret Deal   19

CHAPTER 6

The Fight 22

CHAPTER 7

"Will Bonet Secrecy Pledge"   26

CHAPTER 8

Betrayal!   32

CHAPTER 9

Friends Again   37

A Great Swim

What an amazing dive! He was off the block, curling into the pool like a dolphin.

For a minute, Eddy thought he was seeing things. But, no. It was real. That new boy was ripping along, as if he had been born in a swimming pool. He was so stream-lined under the water that he came up for air out in front of everyone else.

"Pardon me. I'm coming through. Got to get past you here," said Eddy, spinning the wheels of his chair forward. He wanted to get a better view.

"Hey, Eddy, hold on. I'll get you through," said a voice behind him.

Without looking, Eddy knew it was Matilda. They had been friends for years. Matilda liked to chauffeur Eddy around.

"Don't mention her birthday. Don't mention her birthday," Eddy had to remind himself whenever he saw Matilda these days.

He was planning the surprise party of the century with her family. It was still about six weeks away. That seemed like forever when you were keeping a secret.

"Where to, Master Edward, sir?" Matilda asked, putting on her stiff, chauffeur's voice.

"Poolside. On the double," snapped Eddy, craning his neck to see the action in the pool.

"Poolside? Jolly good, sir."

The swimmer in lane 6 had set a fast pace at the beginning. He was still leading, by about five body lengths.

"Look at his style. See how smooth he is, Matilda?" said Eddy, spellbound. "There's very little splash around him."

4

All at once, Eddy saw that the new guy was slowing down. The other swimmers were catching up fast.

The boy in lane 6 finished fourth. It almost looked as if he had done it on purpose.

Eddy wanted to know why.

CHAPTER 2

WILL'S STORY

"What's your story?" asked Eddy.

Laguna Hills' newest student had just finished getting changed. He turned around and saw a boy in a wheelchair, looking very uptight.

"Nobody gets my story until I know their name," he answered, rubbing his wet head with a towel.

"Sorry. I'm Eddy."

"My name is Will."

"Like Will Smith? That's cool," said Eddy. "He's my favorite actor. You even look like him. Or how Will Smith would have looked as a kid."

"So, Eddy, are you a Hollywood agent? You going to make me a movie star?" joked Will.

He nodded to Eddy's wheelchair and asked seriously, "What's with the wheels?"

"I was in a car accident. My legs are paralyzed … for now," said Eddy. "Anyway, I want to help you, Will. I don't want to make you a movie star. I want to make you a swimming star."

"Look, Eddy," Will sighed. "I've heard it all before. I don't care about swimming. I only swam today because that teacher, Ms. Kilpatrick, practically made me. I didn't win. Good. Now she'll leave me alone," said Will.

Eddy leaned forward and said, "Ms. Kilpatrick might leave you alone. But you can't get rid of me. I'm going to help you. And I want to start tomorrow."

CHAPTER 3

A Surprising Turn

"Forget it, Eddy. You wanted my story? Here it is. I'm a twelve-year-old computer nerd," said Will, taking a bow.

"No way!" said Eddy, staring at Will, dumbfounded. "You mean, all you care about is staring at a screen? With your talent in the pool? That's unbelievable!—I just can't—"

"Well, you'd better believe it," cut in Will.

Eddy got very quiet for a moment. Then he carefully said, "You actually *want* to sit around all day, when I have to … I'd give anything to feel my legs kicking through that water. You can't waste your swimming, Will. Please keep it up."

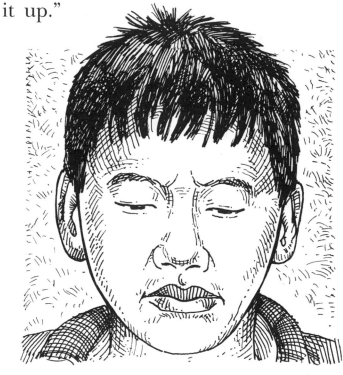

"No!" said Will, firmly.

Eddy didn't flinch.

Just at that moment, they were interrupted by Ms. Kilpatrick.

"Hey, boys. Move it on out. You'll miss the bus," she said. "What are you doing here anyway, Eddy? You should already be on the bus back to school. You didn't swim."

This time, Eddy did flinch, and Will saw it. "Come on, Eddy, let's get out of here," he whispered. "Can I give you a push?"

"I can do it myself," hissed Eddy. "But I still want to talk to you about swimming."

"No way. We're done," insisted Will, racing off in the direction of the bus.

With a quick turn, Eddy's wheels spun forward. His chair went rolling toward the bus so quickly that he overtook Will in no time.

Suddenly Eddy braked, stopping his chair right in Will's path.

Will went flying over the top of him.

CHAPTER 4

A SECRET REVEALED

Will hit the ground, rolling. Fortunately, he landed on the grass, so he wasn't hurt.

"Wow!" said Eddy, impressed. "That was some landing. You could be Will Smith's stunt man."

"Would you stop with the Will Smith cracks? I'm Will Bonet—"

Will clapped his hand over his mouth, looking like he wished he hadn't spoken. But it was too late. His secret was out.

Eddy's reaction was immediate—and huge. "So that's why you lost that race!" he cried. "It all makes sense now. You're Toby Bonet's little brother. You can't stand to be in his shadow. Toby Bonet! He's California's junior state swimming champion," Eddy said, clapping his hands and laughing.

"Yeah, well don't split your sides over it," snarled Will.

Eddy stopped laughing and looked straight at Will.

"What about you, Eddy?" Will asked. "You're all over me about my swimming—but what do you do? Nothing, I bet. Your shoulder muscles are strong, like mine, but your skin's pale. You don't get out in the sun and do things with other kids, do you?" demanded Will.

"No. Because one day, I'm going to be out of this chair …"

"So, in the meantime, you're going to waste time dreaming, instead of doing," said Will. "You're living for the future, Eddy, when you hope to walk. What about today? What are you doing for fun now?"

Eddy didn't answer. In his mind, he saw images of his long stay in the hospital after his accident. The kind nurses. The physical therapist. His parents crying.

Eddy remembered how time had stood still the day the doctor came to see him. He would never forget the way she stalled in the doorway. A bad sign. She had taken off her glasses, twirled them in her hand, and put them back on again.

It had been so quiet as she sat beside his bed. In the silence, words waited to be spoken. Eddy had closed his eyes and listened to the sound of her breathing. It was telling him the darkest news of his twelve-year life.

CHAPTER 5

THE SECRET DEAL

Bus engines could be heard from the parking lot.

Eddy looked up at Will. At last he said, "I can't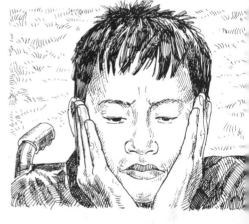

do it, Will. I can't try out for any wheelchair sports. You've got no idea what it was like after that accident. I had to compete with myself so hard to even get used to life in a wheelchair. I can't compete anymore," groaned Eddy.

Will chuckled. "We're the same," he said. "We don't want to try. It's too scary."

"We're not the same, Will. I know you can win," said Eddy.

"Then let's make a deal. I'll enter that big swim meet that's coming up, if right after that, you'll try out for a wheelchair sport," said Will.

He held out his hand to Eddy.

But before Eddy could take it, Will pulled away, saying, "Oh, one more thing. This has to be totally secret. I don't want any of my family to know that I'm going out for the big race. It's just more pressure. I don't want to be compared with Toby."

Will and Eddy shook hands just as Ms. Kilpatrick appeared and said, "Get on the bus!"

CHAPTER 6

THE FIGHT

"Eddy, wait up," a voice called from across the school yard. Eddy spun his wheelchair around to see Matilda coming toward him.

"Don't mention her birthday. Don't mention her birthday," Eddy repeated to himself, and grinned hello at Matilda.

"Where have you been these last few weeks? I never see you," said Matilda, looking hurt.

"I'm watching Will train, remember? The secret," Eddy reminded her.

"Yes, I know—he told me his family can't find out about it. Hey, is your mom driving you guys to the pool after school? I'll come and swim, too."

"Okay. But you'll need to get your mom to take you there, Matilda. See, we have to go somewhere first," Eddy explained.

"Where are you going first?" asked Matilda, in a suspicious voice.

23

"Just to meet some, ah, guys," said Eddy, trying not to sound nervous. "Don't be so nosy!"

"Well, my mom can't take me to the pool. She's got to go and meet some clients at Dad's office, Eddy."

Eddy didn't know what to say. He was trying not to feel guilty. The clients at her dad's office were himself, his mom, Will, and lots of other people.

They were planning an awesome party for Matilda's birthday. This party was going to be big.

"Why all these secrets all of a sudden, Eddy? We never used to keep stuff from each other. If you don't want to hang out with me, just tell me," said Matilda.

"I do. It's just … look, Matilda, I'll catch you later at the pool, okay?" said Eddy, wheeling away.

But Matilda never showed up.

CHAPTER 7

"Will Bonet Secrecy Pledge"

Will's swimming was awesome. Of course, Eddy was at all the training sessions.

"Tell me you're joking! You look like you're swimming through mud, Will, not water! Are you even awake down there?" Eddy would shout, leaning forward in his wheelchair, staring into the deep, blue water.

"Will, I've seen goldfish in a bowl swim faster than you—and they haven't even got arms!"

Sometimes Eddy's mom and the other kids at the pool would tell Eddy to give Will a break. He never did, though. He and Will had made a deal.

Eddy knew that Will could be a champion. He just needed to get over the fear that he couldn't live up to his brother, Toby.

In order to keep Will's training safe from the rest of the Bonet family, Will, Eddy, and Eddy's mom had to let lots of other people in on the secret.

Swimmers had to practically take a "Will Bonet Secrecy Pledge" before they could even dip their big toe in the pool. Management helped, too. Will could train at any time, for free.

As the weeks went by and the big day drew closer, Eddy was really excited about the change in Will's swimming. Every now and then, Will gave Eddy information about wheelchair sports. He wanted to make sure that Eddy was going to keep his end of the deal.

"You can choose any sport, from basketball to swimming," said Will.

"Would I need to wear those floatee things on my legs?" asked Eddy.

"No. Only if you felt unsure in the beginning. But lots of paraplegics like you are swimmers. You just don't use your legs. It's all in the arms, like I told you. So you could train for swimming using weights and stuff. And then, when you compete, they classify you according to your muscle strength and only put you up against swimmers in the same class.

It's going to be so great, Eddy. We'll be able to train together," Will said, slapping Eddy on the back.

"I wish I could talk to Matilda about all this wheelchair sports stuff, Will. But she's real mad at me these days," said Eddy.

"Tell me about it. You know, this secret thing about her birthday party has gotten way out of hand. She's feeling really left out," said Will.

"Well, her birthday is only two days after the swim meet. So all our secrets will be out in the open then," said Eddy.

CHAPTER 8

BETRAYAL!

Will Bonet went into the Southern California Interschool Swimming Competition as the fastest freestyle qualifier at his school.

On the bus ride down to San Diego, a nervous Eddy was giving an even more nervous Will some last-minute advice.

"Listen, Will. In those qualifying heats, you were watching the other swimmers. You can't do that. You've got to race against yourself. You can't be distracted by anybody else in the pool."

However, it was not the other swimmers in the pool who were going to distract Will that day. As they entered the Aquatic Center, Eddy and Will saw that their secret was out. Way out.

Directly under the *Go Laguna Hills!* banner sat the entire Bonet family. But what really surprised Eddy was seeing the person whispering in Toby Bonet's ear. It was Matilda.

"That fink," muttered Eddy. "How could she do it? She knew this race was a big secret from your family."

"That's it, then," said Will. "I'm out of here."

"You're what?" asked Eddy, his jaw open like a trapdoor.

"You heard me. There's no way I can race in front of my folks and Toby. Will you just look up there? I was nervous enough already. I can't get in the pool now," cried Will.

"You've got to," said Eddy, raising his voice. "Remember what I said? Swim your own race. You can't back out now, Will. It's too late. I mailed my letter last night."

"What letter?"

"The letter that goes with the form for the sports camp," said Eddy. "See, I was so sure you'd win today that I was going to keep my end of the deal."

"Oh, no," groaned Will.

Eddy looked at the blue water in the swimming pool.

"We made a deal, Will. And you're swimming today."

CHAPTER 9

FRIENDS AGAIN

While Will was changing and warming up, Eddy sped across the Aquatic Center to get to Matilda. He wanted to tell her a few things about keeping secrets.

Matilda saw Eddy approaching and leaped down the steps to meet him. She had a worried look on her face.

"Why are you guys so late? How come you didn't catch the early bus, like me? Eddy, I've got to explain something," Matilda started, breathlessly.

"No kidding," said Eddy, sarcastically. "How could you do it, Matilda? If you expect me to come to your birthday—"

"Did you see that I arranged for Will's family to come?" asked a voice from behind. Matilda frowned. Eddy turned around to face—Ms. Kilpatrick.

"It's just what he didn't want, Ms. Kilpatrick," insisted Eddy. "You must have heard it was a secret."

But Ms. Kilpatrick had taken off in the direction of the officials.

"That's what I wanted to tell you, Eddy," said Matilda. "I've been asking the Bonets to leave, for Will's sake. But they're so excited, they won't budge."

Eddy looked at Matilda. So she hadn't told Will's secret to the Bonets after all.

But he had let a secret slip, by mentioning the "b" word. Birthday. Matilda's birthday. Two big secrets, both out in one day.

"I'm so sorry, Matilda …"

"It's okay. You just freaked out when you saw me talking to the Bonets. And Eddy—about my birthday—I would love to have you come with us, but my dad said there's only room for my family on the mystery flight. You're not mad, are you?" asked Matilda.

Mad?! No way. The secret was still safe! Matilda had some crazy idea about a mystery flight for her birthday!

Eddy was relieved that he hadn't ruined the surprise. And he was relieved that Matilda wasn't the one who gave away the big Bonet secret.

All of a sudden, Eddy threw his arms around Matilda and hugged her.

"Hey! I don't want any boy germs!" laughed Matilda. "Would you just go and help Will?" she asked.

"You're right. Look! There he is. They'll be called up to the starting blocks any second. I don't have much time," said Eddy, panicking.

Matilda gripped the back of the wheelchair. She smiled and cleared her throat. "Where to, Master Edward, sir?"

"Poolside! And make it snappy."

They got there just in time to see Will do his dolphin routine. His dive off the block was totally amazing.

"Go for it, Will!" shouted Eddy.

At the first turn, Will was so far ahead he could have stopped for a bit of a poolside chat and a photo opportunity and still had time to win!

He burned up the pool, blasting his way to victory. *Everyone* in the Aquatic Center cheered for Will Bonet. And Eddy cheered the loudest of them all.